Annie Rose
is my Little Sister

ANNIE ROSE IS MY LITTLE SISTER
A RED FOX BOOK 0 09 940856 2

First published in Great Britain by The Bodley Head,
an imprint of Random House Children's Books

The Bodley Head edition published 2002
Red Fox edition published 2003

1 3 5 7 9 10 8 6 4 2

Red Fox Books are published by Random House Children's Books,
61–63 Uxbridge Road, London W5 5SA,
a division of The Random House Group Ltd,
in Australia by Random House Australia (Pty) Ltd,
20 Alfred Street, Milsons Point, Sydney, NSW 2061, Australia,
in New Zealand by Random House New Zealand Ltd,
18 Poland Road, Glenfield, Auckland 10, New Zealand,
and in South Africa by Random House (Pty) Ltd,
Endulini, 5A Jubilee Road, Parktown 2193, South Africa

THE RANDOM HOUSE GROUP Limited Reg. No. 954009
www.kidsatrandomhouse.co.uk

A CIP catalogue record for this book is available from the British Library.

Printed in Singapore

For Jack

Annie Rose
is my Little Sister

Shirley Hughes

RED FOX

Annie Rose is my little sister.
She likes books a lot
and she's always wanting me
to look at them with her.

She's quite good at playing games.
She likes it when I hide under a sheet
and pop out at her – Boo!

But when I'm really hiding
she can hardly ever find me.

One of Annie Rose's favourite toys is her little chest of drawers. She likes opening and shutting each one.

She puts all sorts of things inside them.
Sometimes she pulls out all the drawers
and makes them into beds for her
family of mice.

The only things I have in my bed when I go
to sleep are my bit of blanket and my elephant,
Flumbo. He is quite old, nearly as old as me.
But Annie Rose has lots of things
in her cot.

Early in the morning I can hear her throwing them
out on to the floor, one by one – thump, thump,
thump! Then the only thing she has left in there is
Buttercup, her lamb. She doesn't often throw her out.

Annie Rose always wants to play with my toys.
She seems to like them better than her own,
which is very annoying.

When I want to lay out all my cars and trucks
and rail track I have to do it on the table
where she can't get at them.

Our best game, which we play together, is shops. When we have a shop indoors we set out all the little packets and boxes and plastic bottles with screw tops which Mum has saved for us, and we arrange all sorts of nice things on plates from Annie Rose's tea set.

Then I am the shopkeeper, Mr Lewis Burrows, and Annie Rose is my helper.

Sometimes Annie Rose wants to make her own shop
in the back garden. She has leaf plates and sells
empty snail shells and daisy heads.

But she can't make a daisy chain. Neither can I.
Only Mum can do that.

When we go to the seaside Dad and I make a huge
sandcastle with turrets and tunnels and a moat all
around which fills up with water when the tide
comes in. Annie Rose can only make sand pies.
But they are very good ones.

Annie Rose doesn't like the sea much.
She prefers kicking up the water in shallow pools.

But Dad and I like diving into big, rough waves.

Annie Rose can be really awful sometimes. She gets into a rage and lies on the floor and screams and kicks. It is most awful when she does this in a shop.

She usually cheers up again, after a while.

Annie Rose's best friends are Marian and Lily.
They play together a lot. Sometimes – not very
often – Marian and Lily only want to play with
each other and they don't want Annie Rose.
And that makes her very sad.

My best friend is Bernard. When he comes to play at our house Annie Rose always wants to join in. She laughs and laughs when Bernard pretends to be a prehistoric monster, showing its fierce teeth and making terrible noises.

Annie Rose loves Bernard.

But when Annie Rose cries,
or wakes up from her nap
in a cross mood, I'm
the only person who
can cheer her up.

Because she's my little sister,
and I'm her brother,

and we'll go on being that forever...

...even until we're grown-up.